Love on Patrol

Kat Neil

LOWELL STREET
PUBLISHING, LLC

Contents

Prologue

The Beginning

Today was the day Jim was going to ask Tara to be his girlfriend. Four years was a long time to crush on someone. Long gone were the days in third grade when Jim and Tara had played cops and robbers during recess. He had assumed the role of elusive thief, enticing her to pursue him relentlessly across the playground. Jim often outpaced Tara with his remarkable speed, yet, sometimes, he graciously slowed his pace so she could catch up to him. They were just kids back then. Seventh graders didn't play childish games. Jim was ready for Tara to be his lady.

Jim stood at Tara's locker, waiting for her to come within earshot. "Hey, Tara? Can you meet me under the big tree during lunch today? I want to ask you something."

"Why can't you ask me now? I wanted to hang out with Gina and Gabby at lunch," Tara said, gathering her folder and math book from her locker.

"Please? It will only take a minute," Jim begged. He couldn't endure another day of waiting.

Tara stared at him for several seconds before responding to his pleading. "Sure. You got five minutes, max."

"Thanks!" Jim pumped his fist in the air, then ran off to his next class.

In the dimly lit classroom, Jim sat patiently at his desk, his eyes fixed on the clock hanging on the wall. The air was filled with a hushed silence as classmates worked on their assignments. The only sound that permeated the room was the occasional rustle of paper or the soft scratching of pens on notebooks. Jim couldn't focus on his work. He mentally rehearsed what he would say and how he would ask Tara to be his girl. As the seconds ticked away, Jim's anticipation grew.

Finally, the clock struck twelve. Jim rose from his seat and bustled through the classroom door into the hallway. With no time to stop at his locker, he jogged through the crowd and through the double doors, taking the path leading to the tree. There Tara stood, under the tall branches, hands on her hips, scanning the yard. Jim thought she was so beautiful, with her warm cinnamon eyes and big smile. Gasping for air, Jim reached Tara. "Hey," he said, out of breath. "Thanks for meeting me."

Tara impatiently looked at Jim. "What is it? What do you want to ask me?"

Jim took a deep breath, mustering the courage to express his feelings for Tara. His slightly clammy hands only intensified the anxiety he felt. He looked into her eyes, searching for the connection that went beyond friendship. A nervous smile played on his lips. He hesitated for a moment, his heart pounding in his chest. "Will you be my girlfriend?" he blurted.

Tara's eyes widened, caught off guard by the unexpected request. The seconds that followed seemed like an eternity to Jim. Tara took in a breath, then responded, "Sure. Now can I go?" A bewildered expression shown on Jim's face. He nodded. With that, Tara moved closer to Jim.

She beamed, revealing a wide toothy grin, kissed him on his cheek, then ran off to meet her friends.

Each day began with Tara sending Jim a text message. He was awakened by his phone buzzing with a new message notification. Grinning, he grabbed his mobile device and eagerly unlocked it to see a text from Tara.

> **Tara** - Good morning! Meet me at my locker when you get to school.

Jim's heart fluttered as he quickly typed a response. One of his favorite things these days was to wake up to Tara's messages.

> **Jim** - Good morning! Can't wait.

With a contented sigh, Jim tossed his phone to the edge of his bed and rushed into the bathroom to get ready for the day.

As Jim entered the bustling cafeteria, he scanned the room until his eyes landed on Tara, sitting at their usual table near the window. With a grin, he made his way over to her, heart beating fast as he got closer. He didn't think he would ever tire of her beautiful smile.

"Hey, Jim!" Tara said, face lighting up at the sight of him.

"Hey!" Jim said as he sat in the chair next to her.

Together they unpacked their lunches and settled in, the noise in the background fading as they jumped into a lively conversation. They laughed and joked with one another, trading gossip about their friends. Jim pulled his phone from his pocket and began typing a message to Tara.

Jim - You look pretty today.

Tara looked at her vibrating phone sitting on top of the table, smiling when she saw Jim's name flash across her screen. She let out a giggle, then began typing a response.

Tara - Thank you. I like your shirt.

Jim looked up from his phone to see Tara's eyes staring into his. They sat in silence for several moments.

"Can I hold your hand?" Jim asked.

"Yeah." Tara held her hand out for Jim to take it into his. Just as their fingers touched, the bell rang. Lunch was over. Kids began to rush toward the double doors, pushing Jim and Tara along with them.

"I'll talk to you tonight?" Jim asked in a voice louder than normal.

Tara nodded and joined her friends to walk to class.

In the evening, Jim settled in his room, sprawled out on his bed, his phone clutched tightly in his hand. With a quick tap, he dialed Tara's number. She picked up on the first ring.

"Hi."

"Hi, Tara."

"What are you doing?" Tara asked.

"Nothing." Jim wanted to tell her he was thinking about her smile. He always thought of Tara.

For the next hour, they talked about everything and nothing, their conversation switching from the events of the day to their hopes and dreams in the future. Jim told her about the latest episode of COPS and she shared the latest story her dad had shared about his day patrolling the highways. With a yawn, Tara said goodnight. Jim hung up, elated that he and Tara got to spend time together, whether it be at school or on the phone.

Two weeks later, Jim got called out of his science class. It was a Friday. As he entered the office, he saw his dad leaning against the built-in desk, arms crossed, a sullen expression resting on his face.

"Hi, Dad. What are you doing here?"

His father gave a forced closed mouth grin, then said, "Son, we need to go home. I have to share some news."

With that, Jim followed his dad to the car. They sat in silence for a few seconds before his father started his truck's engine, driving the five minutes to their home. When he walked into the living room, Jim knew immediately something was missing. His house felt cold and empty, even though everything was in its usual place. The living room furniture was untouched. The seventy-inch big screen television was still mounted on the wall in the family room. He went to the refrigerator to pull out a bottle of juice and some bread to make toast when his dad spoke.

"Son? Your mother is gone."

Jim stopped and dropped the loaf of sourdough on the island. "What do you mean, Mom is gone? Gone shopping? Gone to Gramma's?"

"No. Your mom decided she wanted to be alone for a while."

What did that mean? Jim's head was suddenly spinning. "Be alone? Is she coming back?" "I don't think so, son. At least not for a while."

Jim couldn't speak. He ran to his dad and wrapped his arms around him. The tears were unexpected. The feeling of sadness and abandonment was immediate.

"Jim, I want you to know that we will be okay. You're my son and I love you. The only way I can explain this is that your mother wasn't happy. She wasn't happy with me. She loves you, though."

People who love one another didn't leave without saying goodbye. Jim knew that much. They stood in the kitchen, embracing one another for what seemed to be a long time. He needed space. "Can I go to my room?"

As Jim sat alone on his bed, the silence seemed to weigh heavy on his shoulders. He stared blankly at the door, willing for his mother to suddenly open it, telling him dinner would be ready soon. Deep down, he knew his mother wasn't coming back. A knot began to form in his stomach, a mix of sadness and confusion swirling inside him. He wanted to pretend that everything was fine, but the ache in his chest wouldn't go away. With a heavy sigh, Jim buried his face in his hands, tears stinging his eyes. The feeling of loss and loneliness overwhelmed him. He needed a distraction. He pulled his phone from his pocket and sent Tara a text.

Jim - Hey.

Seconds later, Tara responded.

Tara - Hey. What's up?

Jim - Not much.

Tara - I looked for you after school.

> **Jim** - My dad picked me up early.

> **Jim** - Do you want to hang out tomorrow?

> **Tara** - Sure. The mall?

> **Jim** - Sure.

Saturday afternoon, Jim stood by the movie theaters; he and Tara's agreed meeting spot. The aroma of fresh popcorn mingled in the air. He checked his phone. It was 2:15. They had agreed to meet at two. It wasn't like Tara to be late. He needed to see her. He needed her smile to warm his cold heart. At 2:30, he sent a text.

> **Jim** - Tara? You still coming to the mall?

The message immediately bounced back, undelivered. He checked his cell service. He had four bars. It wasn't his phone. Maybe Tara was in a no service zone. Jim scanned the crowd headed toward the theater, looking for her. She was nowhere to be seen. He sent his message again, only for it to be returned within one second. He pushed the icon to call her number.

"You've reached a number that is no longer in service," greeted him. Jim didn't understand. He had texted Tara last night. He waited around until four o'clock. He didn't want to go home. Home was a reminder of his mother's absence. Was Tara gone now, too?

For the rest of the weekend, Jim continued to call Tara's phone, only to receive undelivered messages and a voicemail saying the number was no longer in service. On Monday, he waited by Tara's locker. This is what they did every morning. The bell rang, giving him five minutes to get to his first class. Jim's eyes darted eagerly from one end of the hallway to the other, anticipation racing through his veins. He scanned the sea of students hustling to their classes, hoping to see that familiar face. He glanced at his watch, realizing he had one minute to get to class, otherwise he was going to be late. He sighed, then jogged to the far end of the hall and rushed into his math class and sat down.

After school, Jim walked the ten minutes to Tara's house. As he walked down her street, his gaze shifted to her front yard. He stopped in his tracks. A 'For Sale' sign was planted firmly in the front yard. His heart sank as he got closer to it, a sense of disbelief washing over him. He felt the ground shifting beneath him. With a heavy heart, Jim turned in the opposite direction to head home, the sign burned into his mind.

That evening, Jim sat at the kitchen table, his gaze fixed on the empty seat across from him, where his mother usually sat, a hollow feeling settling in the pit of his stomach. Even though he and his dad sat without talking, eating their store-bought dinner, the silence was deafening. He missed his mother's laughter. He yearned for his mother's cooking. Tara's absence left an emptiness that seemed to suffocate him. He missed them both more than words could say. It was as if a piece of him was torn away, leaving behind a raw and gaping wound that would never heal. He wanted to bring his mother back. He wanted Tara to return to school, to sit with him at lunch, hold his hand and tell him everything would be alright. He had to believe that someday, somehow, his life would get better.

Chapter 1

On the Job

Officer Tara Phillips woke up with the first rays of sunlight, and to her phone vibrating off the nightstand with an incoming call. Sheridan's candid snapshot of her slightly opened mouth blowing out her birthday candles, which sat on top of multiple scoops of vanilla, chocolate, and strawberry ice cream and gobs of whipped cream, flashed across the phone screen. Their daily morning wake up call never failed to bring a comforting smile to Tara's face.

"Good morning."

With too much cheer in her voice, Sheridan replied, "Good morning, sunshine. How's my bestie today?"

"Better. Thanks for dinner last night." Tara shifted her body to lie flat on her back. "And for the needed conversation." She could hear Sheridan taking sips of what she knew was a scorching hot cup of coffee, two sugars, and a splash of cream.

"Last night was the first time we had a chance to really talk. Traveling the world opening elite nightclubs for the rich and famous doesn't leave much room for bestie time. Besides, it's time you move on. I hope you can now get back out there. It's been a year, my friend," Sheridan added with much sincerity and truth. Tara believed she was finally ready to put Derek in her past. He didn't deserve the time and space he occupied in her waking thoughts.

Before Derek, there was Giancarlo. Giancarlo entered Tara's life like a fairytale, filled with laughter, shared dreams, and endless affection. In the beginning, their days were woven with joy, each moment brighter than the last. Together, they built castles in the air, imagining a future full of love and happiness. His overwhelming presence wrapped around her like a big hug and brought a sense of completeness. Their bond felt as though it was destined to be. Soon, though, cracks in their relationship were evident. Giancarlo's behavior became unpredictable, leaving Tara unsure of where she stood in his heart. He canceled plans at the last minute without explanation and would often seem distant and aloof when they spent time together. As time went on, Tara became insecure, questioning whether she was good enough for Giancarlo, unsure of their future. The breakup delivered via text message was the final straw, shattering any lingering hope Tara had of their relationship. But it was Derek who tore her heart into tiny shreds. Every reminder of him now taunted her with memories she wished she could forget.

"You know, Sheridan? My breakup with Derek has lingered too long. Our last conversation overwhelmed me with so much disappointment and heartbreak. The bitter reality of us not being together cut through my soul. I thought I was going to marry him."

Sheridan let out a sigh. "I know. It's the ones we fall for the hardest we think are the loves of our lives. Reality punches us in the gut and reminds us otherwise."

Derek was the perfect package. He was an attorney she met during a traffic court case. Their connection, hot and heavy, was like a whirlwind romance, a tempest of passion that swept her off her feet. Tara and Derek's initial encounter was charged with electricity, an accidental collision of souls in a crowded courtroom. What began as a casual conversation quickly ignited into an inferno of attraction.

"He swept me off my feet, all the fine dining, flowers, and good wine. We rushed things. A month is not enough time to commit." Tara now sat up, back rested against her headboard. She wanted to share these last thoughts before never speaking of Derek again.

"A quick commitment is fine with the right person, you know," Sheridan said matter-of-factly.

"We were inseparable. Until he started acting like an ass. It was as if he was bitten by the condescending bug." Tara breathed heavily at the thought of Derek's shift in behavior. His demeanor took a sharp and patronizing turn. He began talking at her instead of with her. He overpowered their conversations. All decisions were his alone. When out in public, he often hushed her words and belittled her.

"He used to say, 'just stand there, look pretty, and don't say a word.' Or, 'I just need you to support me by looking good. You know, be my eye candy.' I should have taken him on a ride-along and pushed him out of the car and onto the crowded freeway."

"Tara! I didn't know you had thoughts like that. Not a bad idea, though." Sheridan laughed.

The night before their final conversation, Tara had stood on the balcony of his luxurious condominium, her gaze lost in the cityscape that sprawled out before her. The city lights twinkled, seeming to dance in celebration of their future that once held so much promise.

"In the back of my mind, I dreaded the thought of Derek being my forever, wondering if this was the right decision. It wasn't clear why I had doubts. I gave him the benefit of the doubt. I was so heart-eyed, I thought he was paying me compliments," Tara admitted.

That night played like a slow-motion movie in her mind. Derek had joined Tara on the balcony, resting his arms on the railing. He took in a deep breath, appearing to appreciate the magnificent view. He then began to speak, never looking at Tara or in her direction. "I'm breaking up with you," he'd said. His words seemed to have been pitched from left field and left Tara speechless. She turned to him, waiting with bated breath for Derek to give her reasons why.

"And his exact words were, 'I don't see a future with you. The demands of your career are too unpredictable. You and your job pose challenges for my future political career.' He had the nerve to say he needed a woman to be one-hundred percent dedicated to him and him only," Tara revealed.

"You didn't tell me that. What a jackass," Sheridan added.

Tara was silent for a few beats. "His words left me devastated and shattered on impact. I thought I loved him."

Sheridan was silent on the other end for a few seconds before speaking. "I didn't know your relationship with him was so unhealthy. You know, you can look back on the ending of your coupledom with Derek as a blessing. There's room now for a real man to cherish you and love you for real, forever."

"You're right." Tara realized it was time to release all her feelings for him and the heartache he had caused. "I'm done, for good."

Tara ended the call with her best friend and went into the bathroom to get ready for her shift. Looking forward to another day on the highway, enforcing traffic laws and ensuring the safety of the roadways. She loved her job. Following family tradition, Tara was the fourth-generation officer to take the oath to keep roads safe, provide service to the public, and offer a sense of security to all who drive the freeways of Southern

California. This legacy of dedication and commitment to public safety ran deep in her family, each generation passing down a profound sense of duty and honor. She followed her great-grandfather, grandfather, and father, who all served with distinction, instilling in her the values of integrity, bravery, and responsibility to the well-being of the community. As she wore the uniform and badge, she felt the weight of their legacy and the privilege of continuing a proud tradition that had safeguarded countless lives over the decades.

Dressed in her crisp, fitted khaki-colored pants and shirt, adorning the bullet-resistant vest, Tara grabbed her handcuffs, taser, pepper spray, firearm, and spare ammunition, attaching it all to her duty belt. She checked her radio, grabbed her baton, and headed out to her patrol car. She loved patrolling the highways on any given day. Her time spent on the job had been a welcome distraction from her broken heart. The rhythmic hum of the engine, the endless stretch of asphalt, and the sense of purpose each shift offered her solace that was hard to find elsewhere.

As Tara hit the road, the familiar drone of the car's motor and the cadent beat of the tires on the asphalt accompanied her thoughts. She maintained a vigilant watch over the bustling traffic, her trained eyes scanning for any signs of trouble. The highlight of this shift was when her keen intuition honed on a vehicle and its erratic movements. With practiced ease, Tara signaled for the driver to pull over, activating her siren in a brief, authoritative burst. Thankfully, the vehicle obediently complied, coasting to a stop on the shoulder of the road.

She stepped out of her cruiser and approached the vehicle, surprised to see a middle-aged woman behind the wheel of the flashy cranberry-red sports car. "Good afternoon, ma'am. Can I see your license, registration, and insurance card?"

With a nod of understanding, the woman said, "I'm going into my purse to get my information. I have to tell you, officer, today is the craziest day ever."

Flashing a hint of a smile, Tara said, "Why is that, ma'am?"

"Today is my final court appearance for my divorce. My soon to be ex-husband is trying to clean my bank accounts, and my attorney is ready to bang the gavel on his nonsense with proof he owes me," the woman said as she handed Tara what she asked for.

Tara completed the necessary checks and then looked at the woman for a few moments. "Ms. Ricci, is it?"

"Yes, officer. My name is Ms. Ricci, but I have to tell you, I'm going back to Rowley. I don't want any thought of him after today."

"Ok, Ms. Ricci, soon to be Ms. Rowley. I'm going to let you off today with a warning. I guess you are speeding because you are running late, and I imagine maybe anxiety of what's to come has you rushing. Please abide by the speed limit and traffic laws. Have a good day."

With a nod of understanding, the woman expressed gratitude and waved goodbye as she pulled away from the side of the road and into the slow lane of the freeway.

For the rest of the day, Tara made routine stops, pulling over drivers for speeding violations, reckless driving, and other infractions. Today, she didn't have to work alongside emergency response teams or coordinate efforts to clear the roadways of hazardous debris. It was a slow day. To-morrow, being her day off, she would sleep in, maybe go for a mani-pedi, and have lunch with her mom.

Just as Tara closed her locker to leave for the night, Officer Turner approached her. "Hey, Phillips? I was hoping you could do me a favor and cover for me tomorrow. Me and the Mrs. want a day without the kids. Her mom is taking them for the day. Can you help me out?"

What do you say to a man who wants to spend time with his wife? Just

ma of a morning pick-me-up brewed from the automatic coffee maker in the kitchen, offering a faint beacon of hope. Jim grabbed a cup and poured the hot brew into it. He slowly pulled the mug to his lips, ready to take a sip, like a weary traveler seeking refuge, hoping the caffeine kick would offer some reprieve from the consequences of the previous night's festivities. A full day of patrolling the streets lay ahead.

The station buzzed with activity as officers prepared for their shifts. Tyler snuck in through the back door and slid into the seat next to Jim, just as the sergeant called his name for roll call. Dark circles under his eyes hinted of little sleep, likely a night filled with all the things that lovers do. Their stolen glances during dinner concealed nothing of he and Nicole's intense romance. Jim could recall maybe two times he was in love. The first time, so many years ago, felt like a distant, dreamlike memory. But was that love at such a tender age? His relationship with Jennifer had been one he thought could have stood the test of time. However, their fate was sealed when she asked him to stop the car on the side of a busy street in San Diego. She got out of the car, and yelled, 'I've had enough of you fearing us. Until you get over your fear that we actually have a future together, we can't be together. I've told you I'm here to stay, but you keep pushing me away and I'm done. Now pop the trunk so I can get my bag. I'll Uber home.' The last he heard, Jennifer was engaged and had moved to North Carolina. Now, his single life seemed to suit him. His mind roamed freely, without the tether of a shared agenda. At this juncture of his life, being single was not a void to fill, but an opportunity to revel in the richness of his own existence. At least, that was what Jim told himself.

The sergeant gave an overview of the day's goals and priorities. "Stone and James? I need you two to back up the guys that are in the middle of a stakeout. Suspicion of a big drug deal going down in about an hour.

You better head out now." Jim and Tyler nodded and gave a thumbs up.

"So, you ready to go out?" Tyler asked as he put on his duty belt.

"Yeah, let's hit those streets. Catch some bad guys," Jim said with a playful twinkle in his eyes.

Jim and Tyler missed the planning and preparation for the drug operation. They only had time to review the outlines the lead investigator slid into their lockers. The objective was obvious. Dismantle the drug operation and prevent more drug trafficking through the Los Angeles streets. Undercover operations revealed the warehouse was a hotspot for meet ups and exchanges of goods. No pictures of key suspects meant there were multiple dealers. The informant tips were what pushed the bust to be today. A big shipment came in last night and a pickup was scheduled in a matter of minutes.

The area was already riddled with drug activity. It wasn't clear why the dealers would pick such an obvious place to swap money and goods. Jim noticed the unmarked vehicles as soon as he turned onto the street. Jim and Tyler were directed to slowly roll down the street, appearing to be cops patrolling the area. As soon as they drove past the unmarked cars, their fellow officers jumped out in tactical gear and bulletproof vests, emblazoned with "POLICE" in bold letters, and began to move with precision. The nearby undercover detectives drew their guns just as the dealer exchanged the drugs with a black briefcase assumed to be filled with unmarked bills. With a swift, coordinated effort, officers, including Tyler and Jim, exited their cars, holding their weapons up to not only the dealers but the cracked open windows, assuming watchmen were on the other side, ready to aim and shoot. Chaos erupted as suspects scrambled to evade capture.

"Stop! Drop the briefcase," yelled a plain-clothed officer from the window inside the warehouse, rifle pointed to fire at anyone who made a wrong move.

"Go in and arrest these guys," the lead detective directed. "We got you covered."

Now, six police cruisers deep, backing them up, Jim and Tyler putting handcuffs on the suspects was a breeze.

"Check the area for more narcotics," another detective directed to the arriving officers. "Let's wrap it up. Jim? Tyler? We'll look for your report on your involvement in today's bust by the end of day."

"No problem," Jim answered.

"Let's get these guys in the car and head back to the station to fill out the paperwork," Tyler said.

By the day's end, the adrenaline rush of the drug bust and arrests had worn off. In the moment, the surge of energy made Jim feel hyper-alert. The crash from it all didn't happen until he got back to the station. A sense of satisfaction, and at the same time, motivation swept over him. His work disrupted criminal activity and potentially saved lives. A bust like this reinforced his commitment to his job and the mission to serve and protect.

Since he was thirteen, the sting of his mother walking out on him and his dad always lingered beneath the surface, leaving him with a persistent fear of being abandoned. He found comfort in the structure and discipline of law enforcement, where each day brought new challenges and the opportunity to make a tangible difference. He would fail the community if he abandoned his responsibilities as a police officer. He didn't want to be like his mother and leave the community or his brothers vulnerable by abandoning his responsibilities as a police officer. The camaraderie with Tyler and the other officers provided a surrogate family, wrapping him in a supportive embrace over the past two years. Protecting the city of Los Angeles gave him a sense of purpose and, most importantly, a way to heal from his past. His life seemed to spiral out of control when his mother left. Through his work, Jim channeled his experiences into a commitment to justice and service, reclaiming control over his life and transforming his fears into strengths, finding a new sense of belonging and resilience.

As the fatigue was setting in, Jim was ready to call it a day and go home. He turned to Tyler, shaking his head. "Tomorrow, I just want to spend the day in front of my big screen, nodding off with a beer in my hand."

"Nicole and I are painting her living room tomorrow, so no rest for me," Tyler shared.

"That's why I live the bachelor life," Jim pronounced. "Have a good night, my friend. See you in a few days." He waved his hand, opened the door, and walked outside, heading to his car.

Chapter 3
Long Time No See

The world outside Jim's window was draped in a tranquil blanket, the hustle and bustle of the city still muted. He quickly dressed in black running pants and a long-sleeved running shirt, to protect him from the morning chill. He laced on his running shoes and stood at his door, mentally preparing himself for his morning run. The door creaked open, the crisp morning air greeting him like an old friend. Jim stretched his arms above his head, then ran in place to wake his muscles. He began with a brisk walk, increasing his pace to a rhythmic jog. The neighborhood, usually alive with activity, remained hushed, with only the occasional chirping of birds or the distant vibration of a passing car.

The rich, sweet, and intoxicating aroma of jasmine filled the air as Jim ran past the garden growing outside the flower shop. He immediately flashed back to his childhood home and the bottle of Chanel No. 5 that sat on the bathroom counter. His mother's perfume. The feelings of that day she walked out overwhelmed him. No matter how hard he tried, he couldn't escape what he never wanted to think about. Does a boy ever get over the day his mother walks out of his life? She claimed she needed to take care of herself, his dad had told him. She'd needed to follow her heart, realize dreams she couldn't with his father. Her unfulfilled personal needs were much stronger than the need to take care of her family. Did she feel she lost her identity? Was the marriage smothering her to the point she lost herself? Did she feel trapped and wanted an escape? She sought a new path, and her journey didn't include him or his dad. The numerous conversations Jim and his father had over the years never managed to answer these questions.

Jim was numb for months after his mother left. What was it about him that made the women in his life leave? His recollection of the day Carly left their shared apartment, with an envelope on the mantle reading "Dear Jim", was etched in his mind. Erika ran out of his house yelling, "Since you're so selfish, only consumed with yourself, be by yourself." Tara had walked out of his life the same time his mother left. Could he count that, given they were only thirteen? She had no control over whether she could stay or go. She could have found a way to reach out to him if she really wanted to, couldn't she? He would have. The thought of anyone else he cared about walking out of his life sent a pang of anger through him. He felt the familiar ache of loss clawing at his heart, uncertain if it could endure another departure. Avoiding relationships shielded him from risk of abandonment and heartache, maintaining a sense of control and self-preservation. Staying single was safe.

Forty-five minutes and seven miles later, Jim stood in his driveway, hands on his knees, trying to catch his breath. Scanning his yard, then his driveway, he noticed the rear tires of his SUV were low. Great, now, a visit to the tire shop was on his agenda for the day. So much for vegging out on the couch in front of the television. Hoping his tires could withstand the journey to the store just a few miles away, Jim quickly showered and dressed for the day, then hopped in his car and headed toward the freeway.

Only a few minutes into his drive, Jim heard a discerning thud behind his car. He glanced at the dashboard, where the tire pressure warning light blinked with urgency. With each inch of movement being a calculated effort to distance his car from the flow of traffic, Jim drove to the freeway shoulder, allowing his car to coast and come to a complete stop. He exited his SUV to find the rear tires were as flat as pancakes. Scuffling back to the driver's seat, Jim pulled his phone from the middle console and called a towing service. As he held the phone to his ear, waiting for the operator, he noticed a highway patrol car stopping behind him.

Jim watched as the highway patrol officer exited the car. Hand resting on the back of the gun that rested in its holster, she approached his side of the vehicle. He rolled down his window, peered up to her, then said, "Hello, officer. I-" She interrupted him.

"I see you have two flat rear tires. Is there a tow service on the way?" she asked.

Jim felt awkward sitting in his car. He was the one who typically approached motorists. He had to get out of the car. "Do you mind if I exit my car? I'm LAPD. I'm going to reach for my badge." Grabbing it from his glove compartment, he held it up so the officer could see it.

The officer stepped back so he could open his door and exit his vehicle.

"Officer Jim Stone," he said, extending his hand as a sign of respect for a fellow officer.

"Officer Tara Phillips," she said, gripping his awaiting hand.

Their eyes locked, and after a few moments, a sense of recognition dawned in his gaze. Still holding her hand, Jim spoke. "Did you say your name was Tara Phillips?" Was this Tara Phillips from elementary and middle school? The one and only he used to play cops and robbers all over the playground?

A slight grin lined her face before speaking. "Jim Stone? Is that you?"

Their handshake lingered, the connection between Jim and Tara refusing to dissipate as they savored the moment, eyes still fixed on one another. "Yes, it's me." Jim couldn't believe his luck. Stranded on the side of the freeway and he ran into his first girlfriend.

"How are you?" Tara asked, displaying a wide smile.

"I'm well. Well, I'd be better if my tires weren't flat. I was just trying to call for a tow truck." Jim said.

"Don't worry about it. I'll radio for a tow truck." But first, tell me, like, what are you doing these days? How long has it been?" They both now stood behind Jim's SUV.

"Almost twenty years. I'm an officer with the LAPD. It's supposed to be my day off, but I was on my way to get my tires fixed." The sun kissed Tara's smooth olive skin. Her presence held him captive. "You?"

"I can't believe I'm talking to Jim Stone. My first boyfriend." Jim could see a laugh bubbling up from within Tara, escaping in a joyful burst of sound. "I've been on the highway for some years now. I started right after college. Tell me, are you married?" As she bit her lower lip, he caught her admiring his muscular physique. It was a good thing he'd shaved this morning. When he was clean shaven, his well-defined Italian features were on full display. Her gaze shifted up to his thick ebony hair. Did she want to run her fingers through it?

Jim scanned Tara from head to toe before locking eyes with hers, which were shaped like almonds, creating an intimate moment. The woman before him represented a significant milestone in his romantic history. The one he never forgot, after all these years. He cleared his throat, not wanting his sudden nervousness detectable in his voice. "No, I'm not married. What about you?"

"Same." Tara said, holding up her empty ring finger, then glanced down at the ground, hiding her now rosy cheeks. Jim flashed a flirtatious grin, eyes suddenly darkened with desire to talk to her, on a date.

"Tara? This may sound crazy, but I would love to take you to lunch, or dinner. Catch up. Are you free later today?"

She studied Jim for several seconds before answering him. "I am. We can meet after my shift if you want. I'm off at three."

He watched Tara give him a once over, then she said, "I'll be right back."

Jim watched her as she walked back to her patrol car, trying not to stare at her perfect ass. Taking a moment to appraise her from head to toe, he couldn't help but notice how she'd matured into a stunning woman. Tara sat, one leg in, one leg out of the driver's side of her patrol car as she used the radio to call a tow service. She exited the car with a business card in hand. With hands in his pockets, shuffling dirt around in a circle, Jim looked up as Tara approached.

"Here," she said, holding out her card with her cell phone number scribbled on the back. "Text me your number and where to meet you."

Jim studied the written numbers in disbelief, marveling at the fact that he finally had a way to reach her. The weight of years of unspoken words pressed down on him. He stepped a little closer, the air between them crackling with tension. Each moment seemed to stretch out like an eternity. As their eyes met, he flashed a devilish smile, and said, "I will."

Chapter 4

Chips, Salsa, and the Stars

As Tara pulled into the station, her phone buzzed with an incoming message. A smile gently tugged at the corners of her mouth. She knew it was a text from Jim.

Jim - Hey! Can you meet me at Carlos' on the Pier at 6:30?

Tara - Hi! Yes.

Jim - See you then.

Tara had just enough time to go home, shower, and drive to the trendy restaurant. She was thankful the restaurant was casual. After a day at work, she lacked the inclination to wear a dress and heels. What if she and Jim wanted to walk on the pier? The eatery had good food, great margaritas, and was on the water. She needed to remember to bring a sweater. Nights on the pier could get really chilly.

Carlos' was packed for a Wednesday night. The lively chatter of patrons filled the air, punctuated by the clinking of glasses and the occasional burst of laughter. Every seat at the bar was taken, with customers leaning in close to converse over the uproar of the crowd. Tara's gaze swept across the crowded room until it landed on Jim, his hand raised in a subtle wave to catch her attention.

With his hands in his dark denim jean pockets, he greeted her with a beaming grin. "I hope this table is okay. Hello, by the way. Please, take a seat."

Tara returned the smile and sat across from Jim, trying not to gawk at his handsome face. He was freshly shaven, the scent of his clean aftershave lingering in the air. His hair was jet black, thick, and nicely styled. She wanted to run her fingers through it. She let her gaze roam across his features, lingering on the sharp angles of his jawline and the intensity of his eyes. Her attention drifted downward, tracing the contours of his fitted black shirt where the subtle definition of his muscles pressed against the fabric. His pants hugged his legs, accentuating their muscular profile.

"This place is busy for a Wednesday night, right?" Tara said, placing her purse down and planting her arms onto the table, watching as Jim took his seat.

"I was a little shocked when I walked in. I flashed my badge to ensure I got us a table. Do you want a drink, water?" Jim asked, signaling the waitress to their table.

"Are we drinking tonight?" Tara wanted to ask, given they hadn't seen each other in years and it was a weeknight. She didn't want to appear too eager.

"Why not? We're celebrating." Jim flashed a playful grin, reading over the drink menu.

"What are we celebrating?" Was it a party running into your middle school boyfriend?

"Old friends seeing one another after so many years and reconnecting." He gave Tara a wink and returned to perusing his menu.

Realization hit Tara. The mere sight of Jim made butterflies flutter in her stomach. She couldn't recall ever feeling this way with just a glance from a handsome man. "Then I'll have a margarita, on the rocks, extra salt along the rim."

"Welcome to Carlos'. Can I take your drink orders?" the server asked, removing a small pad of paper from her apron front pocket.

"This beautiful lady will have a margarita on the rocks, extra salt, and I'll have the same with an extra shot of tequila."

"Excellent. I'll return with your drinks and some chips and salsa." The server studied them for a second, smiled, and walked toward the bar.

"So, Tara. Tell me, what's up?" Jim asked, flaunting a jovial grin.

"These days, I work, go home, and repeat the cycle. You?" She didn't know how to begin a conversation with Jim Stone, her first crush. The last time she saw him was the day before her parents told her they were moving to San Francisco.

"Same." Tara gazed into Jim's eyes as she waited for him to continue his recall of what he's been doing these days. He licked the corner of his lower lip, then said, "I never forgot you, you know."

"Yeah? Well, I never forgot you, either." And she hadn't forgotten him. Jim was her best friend. Until he wasn't.

The server arrived with their drinks and a basket of warm, lightly salted tortilla chips.

Jim raised his glass, directing it in Tara's direction. "To old friends, with hopefully new beginnings."

"Cheers." Tara flashed a shy smile. They clinked their glasses and took big gulps of their drinks. Jim then picked up his shot, nodded to Tara and tipped the glass back, swallowing the tequila in one swig.

"I'm sorry, Jim." Tara suddenly felt eager to apologize for her disappearance back in seventh grade.

"Sorry for what?" He dipped a chip in salsa, then shoved it into his mouth.

"My parents up and moved us to San Francisco without warning. They didn't tell me why either. At least not back then. A reason I didn't know at the time." She picked up her margarita and took another sip.

Jim let out a soft chuckle, then said, "I didn't know what happened to you. We were supposed to meet at the mall. I must have waited for hours. On Monday, I walked to your house and saw the For Sale sign in your front yard. I realized that was out of your control."

"It was. You were my best friend, Jim." Tara felt her voice beginning to tremble. As their eyes met, a rush of emotions flooded her senses, transporting her back to a time when her heart seemed to beat in rhythm with his. Their tender moments surged forward, overwhelming her with a bittersweet nostalgia.

Without dropping his gaze, Jim spoke. "And you were mine." For several seconds, they sat at their table, the sound of boisterous conversations and cheering around them, relishing in the moment. Tara took another sip of her drink, then revealed, "We had to move."

"What do you mean you *had* to move?" Jim asked.

"My dad was a highway patrol officer. Do you remember that?"

Jim nodded.

"Well, my dad testified in a serious case. A guy he pursued on a high-speed chase. My dad's squad car cornered him. He jumped out and tried to run, but my dad shot him in his foot to disable him. He thought if it wasn't for my dad, he would have gotten away. He began threatening him. He found out where we lived and threatened my whole family. Dad didn't want to take any chances, so he moved us, changed all of our accounts and cell phone numbers and moved us to northern California." Tara dipped a chip into the salsa and took a bite.

"What happened to the guy?"

"He was sent to prison on the already filled rap sheet of federal crimes and charges he was running from. His actions toward my dad and us added to his time. Life without the possibility of parole." Tara realized she was playing with her drink, swirling her straw around the rim of the glass. She looked up at Jim and gave him a faint smile that spoke volumes of the memories and emotions shared between them before her disappearance.

Jim extended his hand across the table, reaching out for hers with a tender urgency. As their fingers intertwined, he gave her hand a gentle squeeze, conveying a reassurance that went beyond the gaps of time and distance.

"Thank you for sharing that." Jim lifted his glass, prompting Tara to do the same. Their eyes locked in a silent acknowledgement of the moment's significance. They nodded at one another, clinked their glasses, and took a sip of their drinks. "But you know what? We're all grown up now, and we could be best friends again. Maybe more." He flashed her a seductive smirk.

For the rest of dinner, Tara and Jim talked about their high school years, college, and what it was like to be officers of the law. After the bill was paid, Jim stood, reached for Tara's hand, and led her out of the restaurant.

"Wanna take a walk on the pier?" Jim asked, standing directly in front of Tara, close enough to feel her hair brush his face with the gust of wind.

Tara looked up and into his eyes. "Sure." She interlocked their fingers and began slowly walking down the pier. It was a chilly night. Not many people were outside. She didn't care. She had missed Jim. It was an odd thing to feel, given she only remembered the thirteen-year-old Jim. But in his eyes and his laugh, she saw the same bold, passionate kid who asked her to be his girlfriend.

They strolled to the end of the pier in silence. The sun had set, and the water was dark. The sound of the lapping water soothed Tara's senses and calmed her nervousness at being so close to Jim. The only light shining was the tall lamp which lit their path. Jim turned to her, released his hand from hers, and brushed the back of his hand along her soft cheek. "Can I take you out, Tara Phillips? Like on a real date?"

Tara stared into Jim's dark chocolate colored eyes, slowly shifting her gaze up to the sky, then back to him, stars casting their light, illuminating his handsome features. "Yes, I would love to go out with you, Jim Stone."

Chapter 5

New Beginnings

Each morning, Tara's phone buzzed with Jim's messages, the screen lighting up with his familiar words that brought a smile to her face. The sound of his voice, warm and comforting, was a daily ritual she looked forward to. She could almost feel his presence as they shared stories, hobbies, interests, and the expectancy of their upcoming date. Each contact made her heart flutter with anticipation. On video calls, he relished her laugh, the cute way she wrinkled her face when he shared a peculiarly strange story from the day's beat. Once, Jim and Tara found themselves following the same suspect on a freeway high-speed chase. They could only wave, both in heavy pursuit to capture the wanted criminal.

"Who is that?" Tyler curiously asked as Tara sped past them. He hadn't seen Jim blush like he did, ever.

"My new beginning," was all Jim shared.

It was rare for Jim to have a Saturday night off. Tara called in a favor to get out of work. As he stopped in front of her house, a wave of excitement washed over him, making his heart race with anticipation. He couldn't recall the last time he felt this keyed up about a date. But it was Tara Phillips. His thirteen-year-old self wouldn't believe they were really going on a grown up date. Jim stepped out of the car, inhaled a deep breath, and emptied his lungs with a loud exhale. Unexpectedly, nerves crept in, unsettling him. This was definitely new.

Tara opened her door, and Jim's breath caught in his throat. She stood there, illuminated by the soft glow of the porch light, looking absolutely stunning. The sight of her left him momentarily speechless. Her style, classy yet sexy, was ravishing. He took her in, lavishing the way her black dress hugged her toned, curvy body. Her curls appeared soft, cascading down to her shoulders in gentle waves that framed her beautiful tan-colored face. Jim's eyes traveled slowly from Tara's head to her toes, stopping at her black strappy heels which exposed her white smokey manicured toes. His eyes wandered back up her body, pausing when he reached her radiant face.

"You look gorgeous," Jim said in a low sultry voice.

"Thank you. You don't look so bad yourself." Tara walked toward him, running her finger along his jawline. Jim gently grabbed her wrist, bringing her hand up to his face, holding it there for several seconds, staring into her eyes, communicating what was on his heart. Tara slowly removed her hand from his grasp, her fingers lingering for a moment before slipping away, leaving a tingling warmth where they had touched. She turned into her entry way to grab her purse and keys. "You ready?"

Jim blinked several times to jerk himself out of the stupor her beauty put him in, and said, "Yes. Let's go."

Jim stopped in front of the upscale dinner and jazz club, opening his door to hand the valet his keys, then rushing to the passenger side to help Tara out of his SUV.

"I've wanted to come here for a while." Tara glanced up at Jim, grinning as she grabbed his arm to walk into the restaurant and said, "I'm glad I'm with you." Her words carried a weight of sincerity as she met his gaze with a small, genuine smile.

As they walked up to the hostess table, Jim pulled out his badge and said, "We have a reservation for two."

"Good evening, Mr. Stone. You are in good company tonight. There are a few of your fellow officers dining with us. Let me show you to your table." She grabbed two menus. "Follow me."

"Oh yeah? Other officers in a romantic place like this tonight?" Jim snickered. Tara shook her head, holding her lips tight, fighting off the urge to laugh out loud.

As the hostess showed them to their table, Jim couldn't help but lower his eyes to watch Tara as she subtly swayed her hips as she walked. Her stride ignited a flame of desire within him. As they wandered into the restaurant, Jim noticed the ambiance. It was sophisticated and intimate. The venue was adorned with warm lighting that hung from the ceiling, dark wood tables dressed in crisp white linens, and plush red velvet chairs. A subtle scent of aged oak mingled in the air with the tantalizing fragrance of freshly prepared meals. The exposed brick walls and timeless, smooth jazz tunes transformed the space into a sensual haven.

"I'm impressed, Jim," Tara whispered across their table. "This place is nice, sexy, even."

"Sexy, huh?" At the mention of sexy, Jim raised an eyebrow in intrigue. Tara flashed him a seductive smile before opening her menu.

Sitting back in her chair, Tara looked over his face, licking her lower lip when her eyes landed on his mouth. Glancing back up into his eyes, she said, "You look good."

Jim coughed into his napkin, face reddening at her compliment. "Well, I... I... thank you? Hold that thought. For later." He felt a mixture of surprise and pleasure at Tara's compliment. A flicker of happiness ignited, savoring the affirmation of her words.

"I don't know about you, but I'm starving. Do you see anything that looks good?" Jim peered over the menu, eyeing a ribeye steak with lobster macaroni and cheese.

"Everything looks so delicious. I'm thinking about the grilled salmon," Tara said.

Jim settled on a hearty steak cooked to perfection, accompanied by a side of garlic mashed potatoes and steamed asparagus. Tara ordered a vibrant salad bursting with crisp greens and colorful vegetables, tossed in a tangy vinaigrette. Her salmon was infused with a hint of citrus and herbs.

Jim sipped his wine and gazed at Tara. "I'm really glad we could do this tonight. It has been such a busy week."

"Me too. It's nice to unwind and have some quality time together," Tara replied, toying with her wine glass. "How was your day?"

"It was good, but I've been looking forward to tonight all day. We busted a prostitution ring today, and I finally finished all the reports. This is a perfect way to end the week. How about you?"

"Well." Tara took a deep breath, "I think my boss is up to some shady shit, and I hope not to get roped into it." She didn't really want to talk about work. She was on a date. Changing her mood, Tara licked her bottom lip, gave Jim a seductive smile. "I'm thrilled to be here, with you, in this cozy, sexy restaurant. The perfect way to cap off the week."

Jim sat back in his chair, eyes blazing into Tara's. "You're becoming my best friend. You know that?"

"You mean your best friend again, right? We used to be close, tell each other everything. Talk all the time." Tara stared at Jim for a few seconds before taking a sip of wine.

"Since we reconnected, I feel like a giddy kid again. Is that weird?" Jim asked.

With a little chuckle, Tara said, "Me too. It's a good feeling."

"I have to admit, you are beginning to mean a lot to me, Tara."

"I care about you, too, Jim."

They sat at their table for several moments, looking into each other's eyes, Jim's eyes growing dark and hungry to get closer to Tara. He stood and walked over to Tara, reaching for her hand, pulling for her to stand, then led her to the dance floor. It was filled with couples swaying to the contemporary jazz the band played. He pulled her into him, moving to the music with ease and skill.

"You can dance, Jim. Where did you learn moves like that?" Tara rocked to his tempo, resting her hands around his neck.

"Don't laugh, but I joined the jazz club in high school to impress a girl." Jim took delight at the flashback.

Tara looked up at him and let out a gentle laugh. "Well, if you see her again, tell her thank you."

Without warning, the music slowed down to the hum of an instrumental version of Ribbon in the Sky, originally sung by Stevie Wonder. Jim pulled Tara close, holding her hand in his, resting on his chest, the other resting on her waist. With her other arm around his neck, Tara rested her head on his chest, feeling the vibration of his beating heart. They surrendered to the song, letting it envelop them in its embrace, anchoring them in the present. Jim brought his face close to Tara's, sensing the warmth radiating from her skin. They stayed in that position for several moments. He then lifted his head and tilted her chin to meet his gaze. Their eyes locked, both sensing the yearning to succumb to a kiss. Jim slowly lowered his lips to hers, lightly brushing a kiss on them. He could feel her whole body begin to tremble. He tightened his hold on her, then smiled against her mouth. Feeling her grin, he kissed her gently before dipping his tongue between the seam of her lips. Tara opened her mouth, inviting him in, deepening their kiss. Sudden awareness of no music playing brought them out of their haze. Jim, still holding Tara, lowered his lips to her ear and whispered, "Tara, will you be my girlfriend?"

Tara looked up at him and said, "Yes, I will be your girlfriend," then gave him a kiss on the cheek.

Chapter 6

Triggers

Tara's eyes were glued to the passing scene as she and Jim took the long drive to the restaurant. A mesmerizing panorama of blue hues and shifting light appeared in sight. Waves crashed against the shore in a relentless dance, their foam-tipped crests glinting in the sunlight. Seagulls swooped and soared overhead, their cries mingling with the soft sounds of the smooth jazz that played on the car stereo. She rolled down the window, letting the salty breeze kiss her skin. The vista of the ocean captivated her senses, drawing her gaze to the endless expanse of deep blue stretching out before her.

"This drive is breathtaking. How did you find this route?"

"Tyler and Nicole often take this drive. His recommendation. I take it, you like it?" Jim glanced over at Tara as her hand hung out of the car window, capturing gulps of air in her palm. A sudden shift of wind blew her soft curls into her face. He reached over, gently stroked her hair, then tucked strands behind her ear. "Do you want to stop? We have time to kill before our reservation."

"Yeah, let's stop." Tara's eyes traveled along the rugged coastline, admiring the extensive views of the majestic cliffs and azure waters stretching out into the horizon. "That would be nice," she said in an alluring drawl.

Jim pulled into a spot overlooking the water, the car coming to a gentle stop with a perfect view of the shimmering surface. The sound of the water lapping against the shore created a soothing backdrop, adding to the romantic ambiance of the moment. As the sun began to dip below the vista, he turned to Tara. "Have I told you how beautiful you are today?" He unbuckled his seatbelt and reached for her hand, drawing it to his lips, brushing a soft kiss along her knuckles.

Tara closed her eyes, allowing herself to savor the sensation of Jim's lips on her hand. She dreamed of the day his lips would be all over her body. "No, you didn't tell me how beautiful I am today, but your kisses remind me of that very fact."

Jim twisted his upper body to get closer to Tara. He clutched her chin, drawing her face to his. She could practically taste the minty scent that escaped his mouth. She couldn't wait. Her hands pulled his face to hers, and then her mouth was on his, in a rushed, heated, deep, and sensual kiss. He moaned into her, softly nipping her lower lip before licking it to soothe the bite. Tara lifted her body and shifted so her back was to the window, stretching her leg over his lower body to straddle him. "Tara," Jim groaned as his hands began to explore her upper body. Her skin was warm and soft. She planted kisses on his neck, breathing him in as she began to gyrate her hips, feeling the growing bulge in his jeans. "Slow down, baby. We can't let our first time be in the car."

As if Tara was shaken awake, she looked into Jim's eyes. "What?"

Jim began to peck behind her ear, then whispered, "Tara, I want you so bad. I need you."

"I know. I want you, too." She nestled herself into his lap and kissed him again, this time teasing him with her tongue, caressing his pecs as he cupped her breasts. He felt her nipples harden as he drew circles around them.

"Fuck, Tara. I'm trying to hold on here. Can we stop? Please?" Jim let out a gentle moan as he laid his head back on the headrest.

Tara sank in defeat, kissed Jim on the cheek, and returned to her seat. "Can you see out the window? They're a little fogged up."

At that moment, Jim looked at the windshield to see a thin layer of mist obscuring the view outside. "We should go to the restaurant." Jim started the car, turned on the defrost, and turned to take in Tara's warm eyes. "I want to be the utmost gentleman. I swear, but you are making it so fucking hard."

She flashed Jim a devilish grin and nodded. "Our day is coming. No pun intended."

Ten minutes later, he drove into the restaurant's parking lot. A crowd surrounded the entrance of the restaurant.

"What's going on?" Tara wondered out loud.

"Let's find out. We have a reserved table, so we shouldn't have to wait." Jim parked the car, exited it, then met Tara on her side. Arm in arm, they walked through the crowd.

"Excuse us. Excuse me," Jim said to patrons as he guided Tara through the crowd. He saw people grouped around the hostess table. "Stay here and be beautiful. I'll see what's going on."

In an instant, Tara froze. Did she hear Jim correctly? Did he just tell her to stay there and be beautiful? Her mind immediately flashed to Derek, saying those exact words, his tone dripping with condescension. She could almost hear his dismissive voice, see the impatient flicker in his eyes as he waved her concerns away. The memory stung, a reminder of how he had always treated her as if she were incapable of handling anything on her own. Not only did frustration churn within her as she recalled Jim's rejection from her advances, but his recent comment felt like salt in the wound. He dismissed her, making her feel small and unimportant. The emotional belittlement left her seething with anger and hurt. It burned in her chest.

"What did you just say?" Tara 's face flushed a deep crimson, heat radiating from her cheeks as anger surged through her veins.

"What?" Jim asked, not sure what the problem was. "I asked you to stay here so I can check on the table."

Her eyes narrowed, and her jaw clenched tightly, every muscle in her face tense with the vigor of her fury. "I can take care of myself, and I do have a voice. I can also speak for myself." Tara's eyes shot fire at Jim.

"I didn't say you couldn't. What's going on, Tara?" Jim was confused. He didn't know what shifted her mood.

"I wanna go. Take me home. Now, please." Tara stood with her arms crossed over her chest.

"Okay?" Jim paved a way for them to walk out of the restaurant. He helped Tara into the car, got in, then looked at her. Tara knew the stern look on her face was enough for him to not say a word. She turned her body away from Jim and looked out the window, stewing in her thoughts. It was Derek who made her feel small and undervalued. She hoped for respect and equality from Jim and their relationship. A huge shadow now cast over their precious moments. Moments she cherished. Did he see her as less capable? Was that who Jim was? A man who saw her as an object, or a woman who couldn't take care or do for herself? They drove the long way to her house in complete silence.

Jim sent text messages and called, but Tara didn't have the strength to respond to him. Every time she thought about spending time with him, the sting of his condescension resurfaced.

"Tara?" Sheridan said. "Do you think you're overreacting?"

Tara stared down, watching her fork flip through her salad. She wasn't hungry anymore.

"Based on what you've told me, Jim is not Derek. And it's not fair to compare him to your asshole ex boyfriend."

"You didn't hear what he said." Tara couldn't look at Sheridan. She knew she was right. But Sheridan didn't know how deep that comment had cut through her. It planted a seed of doubt, growing a barrier that made the idea of seeing him unappealing. The warmth and excitement she once felt were now overshadowed by a sense of unease and reluctance, compelling her to reconsider the relationship altogether.

"Don't you think you owe him a conversation, Tara? Jim isn't some man you just met. He was your first boyfriend. And now you won't return his calls or answer his text messages?"

"Sheridan? Please let me deal with this my way." Tara wasn't ready to face the facts that were slowly becoming undeniable. She pushed down the uncomfortable truths, unwilling to confront the reality of her feelings. Admitting the full extent of her emotions felt too overwhelming. Right now, she chose to bury her thoughts and fears and live in the fragile comfort of denial. The denial that she hadn't fully processed her relationship with Derek, and she was now holding Jim responsible for the pain her ex boyfriend inflicted.

Chapter 7

Confessions

In the quiet of her time alone, memories of Derek flooded Tara's mind, each one a painful reminder of the toll their relationship had taken on her sense of self-worth. She recalled the countless times he had made her feel small, dismissed her opinions, and silenced her voice with his arrogance. It wasn't Jim who left her feeling disempowered and unheard—it was Derek. The weight of those memories pressed down on her, a much too heavy burden to carry any longer. She knew she needed to reach out to Jim.

Tara stood to leave the briefing room when she heard her captain speak.

"Phillips! Turner! Stay. I need a word with you both," Captain Hanson demanded.

In unison, Phillips and Turner replied, "Yes, sir!"

Tara avoided interactions with her supervisor at all costs. Much like Derek had done in the past, her supervisor's words cut deep, leaving her feeling invalidated and invisible in the workplace. His dismissive comments reverberated in her mind, each one a sharp reminder of her perceived insignificance. Just as Derek had made her feel small and unheard in their relationship, her supervisor's words served to diminish her confidence and sense of self-worth in the professional realm. It was her oath and not only her commitment to her job and community, but her legacy she was determined to uphold. With mighty determination, she refused to let her supervisor tarnish the legacy she and the men in her family had worked so hard to build. Determination burned bright within her. She had to work on reclaiming her voice, to assert her strength and resilience in the face of adversity.

In Captain Hanson's office, Tara and Officer Turner sat quietly, waiting for the ball to drop. "You two! I need you to circulate the 5 freeway. There are rumors of a sniper hidden in the mountains along the roads. This suspect has already fired at passing cars. No one has laid eyes on this person, but they are out there. Your presence will hopefully slow his actions and intent until the LAPD can catch him."

Turner turned to Tara, giving her a questioning gaze. "With all due respect," Turner spoke. "Isn't that dangerous? We would be at great risk, being the only officers in the area. We would be targets, taxing the area."

"This isn't an option, Turner. This is a directive. When on duty, you two will survey the area while keeping our highways and travelers safe." His stare was overbearing. He had a mind of his own.

Tara knew she had to say something. "Sir, it's against policy for Officer Turner and me to isolate ourselves without back up from the LAPD."

"Don't question my authority, Officer Phillips. And I know what the dangers are. If we play an integral part in the sniper's capture, our division will stand out, and it will support my run for commissioner." With that, a frown deepened the furrows between his eyebrows. "You both are dismissed. Oh, and this begins on your next shift."

Pushing open the door to the locker room, Tara looked around to see if anyone was nearby, then whirled to face Turner. "You know this puts us in great danger, right?"

Turner sat with his head in his hands. "Yeah, and he didn't even consider your warning."

"My boyfriend is LAPD. I'm gonna talk to him. Captain Hanson can't get away with this." At the mention of 'her boyfriend', Tara knew what she had to do.

Tara drove straight to Jim's house after her shift, hoping he would be home. She needed to release the heaviness she felt in her chest. The weight pressing in that area was the visceral reminder of the emotional load that would lighten after she told him the truth. Captain Hanson was a different story. But she knew Jim was a man who cared about her and viewed her as an equal. He would never push her aside, dismiss her, or not validate her, her feelings or words. The realization settled within her like a quiet but profound revelation. She knew it now, deep in her bones, with a certainty that she could no longer ignore. She now embraced the truth of her own strength and resilience. Jim was not Derek. She was ready to face Jim with the truth.

Tara took in a deep breath before pressing the doorbell. After not hearing movement, she pushed on the doorbell again.

"Hold on," she heard Jim say. His face appeared at the window, peering out to see who rang. Surprise washed over his face, evident in the sudden widening of his eyes and the parting of his lips. He disappeared from the window to open his door.

"Hi! What are you doing here?"

Tara knew that was a fair question to ask. A month had passed with no contact. "Hi! Can I come in? We need to talk."

Without saying a word, Jim opened his door wide so Tara could walk in. He closed the door behind her. "Do you want to sit down?"

As she stepped into his house, Tara couldn't help but feel a sense of appreciation at how impeccably neat and organized his house was. The scent of lavender engulfed her senses as he led her to the open kitchen and family room. There wasn't a speck of dust in sight. His big screen television displayed a game in progress, the ESPN ticker running across the screen with the latest sports news. A half empty beer bottle sat on top of a coaster and an open bag of pretzels rested on the coffee table.

"I didn't mean to interrupt your day. I wasn't sure if you'd be home, but I had to come." Tara sat at the edge of the oversized dark gray sectional couch that took up most of the space.

"What's up? Can I offer you a beer? Water?" Jim walked to his stainless steel refrigerator.

"Water's fine." Tara nervously rubbed her hands together, uncertain of where to start or what to say. Jim set her water on the table, then sat a few feet away from her on the couch.

"Let's talk shop for a minute," Tara said, looking at Jim.

Jim faced Tara, straightened his back and rested his arms on his thighs. "Okay, we're talking shop."

"Do you know anything about the sniper that is supposed to be in the mountains off the 5 freeway?"

A look of puzzlement etched across Jim's face, furrows formed on his brows. "Sniper?"

Tara let out a breath. "My captain got wind of a sniper that may be in the mountains and charged me and my colleague to that territory while on duty. Said we can help the LAPD. Said shots have been fired, targeting passing motorists."

"That's not your duty. I mean, sure, you patrol the highways, but you don't investigate anything like that. That puts you in harm 's way. I can't believe your captain would set you up like that."

"Right? Do you have buddies that patrol the streets near the 5? I'm on duty next week, and I'm certain he'll make that my assignment. Turner, my colleague, said that's been his beat this week."

Jim stood to his feet and took a few steps around the couch. "I'll find out. I don't like this at all, Tara."

Tara looked down at her hands in her lap. "What do I do?"

"When you go back to work, text me. I'll find out who's in your area. In the meantime, I'll snoop around to see if this sniper story has any teeth."

Tara watched Jim pace the length of the back of the couch. "Sit down, Jim. Please?" Tara could feel her anxiety mounting as she prepared to disclose what burdened her thoughts. "I owe you an explanation and an apology." Tara lifted her gaze from her feet to Jim's intense stare.

"Okay. Say what you have to say." Jim sat and pressed his back against the couch cushion and faced her.

"I was in a relationship a while back. An unhealthy one." Tara began to fiddle with her fingers, not knowing how to continue. Jim closed the distance between them, sensing her nervousness. "In the beginning, everything was good. But then after a while, he began to belittle me, treat me as if I was invalid, not important. He silenced me. Told me to just be beautiful and not to talk." Jim's eyes widened with apparent recognition, his own words insinuating the same sentiment. He lowered his gaze and nodded in agreement, understanding.

"When I heard you say what you said back at the restaurant, it triggered me. I instantly became angry and shut down." Tara was looking at Jim now, eyes brimming with tears, threatening to spill over at any moment.

"Why didn't you tell me about your previous relationship?" Jim moved closer, grabbing Tara's hands to hold in his.

"I didn't think it mattered and didn't want to stir up the past. I felt like what we had was the start of something amazing. You were great. You are great. I missed you."

Jim looked into Tara's eyes, appearing to search for what he didn't know. "I'm happy to see you." He stroked a hand against her cheek.

Tara stayed silent, shaking her head.

"I sent text messages, left voicemails. I kind of felt a sense of loss, not seeing you, Tara." Jim took a deep breath before speaking. "There's something I need to share with you too."

Tara looked up at Jim, swallowing and slowly nodding for him to continue.

"When I didn't hear from you and couldn't get a hold of you, I got really scared. I thought you left me. Like when we were kids." Jim gently squeezed Tara's hands, as if gathering strength to continue his story.

"My mom left me and my dad when I was thirteen. Actually, the day before you moved away."

Tara looked up at Jim, eyes welling with tears, a sudden rush of emotions threatening to spill over.

"That was the worst day of my life. I felt instantly abandoned, lost. And to be honest, unloved. What mother leaves her child. Susan Stone was the one woman who was supposed to love me unconditionally, be present in my life. I didn't even understand what happened. For a minute, I felt like you were abandoning me again. Your absence triggered me."

"Oh, Jim. I'm so sorry." Tara could no longer hold her tears.

"Our rekindled friendship means so much to me. I don't want to lose you."

Without pause, Tara rushed Jim, enveloping her arms around his neck, resting her head on his shoulder. He wrapped his hands around her waist and pulled her in for a tight hug. "Baby. I hope you know you can always talk to me. You don't have to hold anything back. And I won't hold back either."

Tara let her tears fall, sniffling into Jim's neck before speaking. "I won't hold back anymore. Can I kiss you?"

Jim pulled back to gaze into her damp eyes. He kissed her soft lips tenderly, then kissed the tears running down both cheeks. Pressing his forehead to hers, he inhaled her heavenly floral scent, burying it into his memory.

Tara's mouth began to tremble. "I can't believe your mom left you and your dad. That's terrible. I am so, so, so sorry. I'm sorry that happened to you." She pulled him into a blanketing hug.

They stood, holding each other for several beats. Jim then said, "Promise you won't leave me?"

"Never. I will never leave you, Jim."

Jim sighed in relief. "If we're going to be together, we have to share everything. Not hold back. Anything."

"I know." Tara nodded.

They stood in an embrace for several more minutes, not saying anything to each other. Then Jim asked, "Tara? Can I take you away for a weekend? Get out of the city?"

"Yes, let's go."

Chapter 8

Two Hearts

Tara decided to wait in the car while Jim checked into their room. He sensed her nervousness as they got closer to their destination. He, too, felt a nervous flutter in his chest. This was their first weekend trip together. Jim surveyed the grand lobby entrance as he walked to the registration desk, with polished marble floors, plush furnishings, and sophisticated décor. The rich aroma of fine wine tickled his nose. The large windows offered sweeping views of colorful manicured gardens and the vineyards bathing in sunlight and rolling hills blanketed the grapevines. The picturesque view created a sense of tranquility and serenity. It was exactly what he wanted for them on their first weekend alone.

"Hello. Welcome to Moon Trails Winery and Resort. How can I help you?" The woman at the first desk greeted him with a warm smile.

"Yes, I have a reservation for the weekend. Jim Stone," he said, pulling his wallet out of his pocket.

"Yes, Mr. Stone. I see your reservation. You reserved two nights in the Sonoma suite. I'll just need a card to put on file, your ID, and then you'll be all set."

Jim handed the woman his credit card and driver's license, then asked, "Do you see my dinner reservation for tonight at 6:30?"

"Yes, you'll be dining in our five-star restaurant. Our James Beard award-winning chef will have a variety of delicious specials sure to delight even the most discerning taste buds. I'm sure you will have an exquisite meal. Here are your room keys, your parking tag, and a brochure highlighting our wine tours and tasting packages. Is there anything else you need at this moment?"

"No, this is great. Thank you." Jim walked back out to his car and saw Tara standing nearby, admiring the scenery.

"This place is gorgeous. You outdid yourself, Jim." Tara turned to him and wrapped her hands around his waist, giving him a squeeze.

"Let's get our things and go up. We can plan our wine tours and tastings for tomorrow. We have dinner reservations this evening." Jim still couldn't believe Tara was his girlfriend. After the day she had apologized for her coldness and he had shared his mother leaving him and his dad, it was as if the floodgates opened to deepen their connection and care for one another. Their conversations flowed with newfound openness and authenticity. Their work schedules were grueling, though. Sometimes, all they could do was talk. He yearned to see her, hold her, just be in her company. He was falling for her.

"You booked a suite?" Tara said, turning in a slow circle as she took stock of their accommodations. The room opened to a large living room surrounded by floor to ceiling windows that overlooked the vineyard. She walked from one room to another, then glanced over at Jim, with an astonished look. "You booked a two-bedroom suite?"

"I didn't want to assume we would be sleeping in the same bed. We're boyfriend and girlfriend, but we haven't had *that* talk. I didn't want to come off like an ass, presuming we were doing that." Jim scrutinized her expression, searching for clues showing how she felt about their weekend together. Would they share a bed, share one another? He hoped so, but he wanted Tara to be ready, comfortable.

Tara closed the distance between them, reaching for his hands, interlocking their fingers. "I appreciate your thoughtfulness and guardedness, not assuming this was that weekend. Let's see where things go." She then tilted her head to gaze into Jim's eyes, seeing the desire build, turning his pupils large and dark. She pressed her lips on his, giving him a sensual kiss. He deepened the kiss, hands caressing her back. Tara moved her hands from around his neck to run her fingers through his soft, thick, ebony hair. He pulled away, letting out a whimper. "Tara," he whispered, lowering his head to brush kisses along her jaw and neck. She tilted her head back, giving him full access to devour her. He slowly walked her to the couch, wanting to lie her down to take this make-out session to another level, when they were interrupted by a knock on the door.

"Just a minute," Jim shouted, shrugging his shoulders to indicate he didn't know who was there or why. He straightened his clothes, ran a hand through his hair, then opened the door.

"Mr. Stone," a server said, standing in the doorway, handing him the contents in his hands. "A bottle of our sparkling wine. Compliments from Tyler and Nicole."

Jim took the glasses, bottle, and card. "Thanks!" He then reached in his pocket and pulled out a five-dollar bill and tipped him.

"What's that? And who are Tyler and Nicole?" Tara asked, confused. "Oh. Tyler is your partner right?"

Jim set everything down in the kitchenette and opened the card. It read:

To a fantastic weekend. Happy for you! Tyler and Nicole

He let out a chuckle and shook his head. "Yes, Tyler is my partner. He and Nicole are good friends of mine. I mentioned we were going away for the weekend. Our first weekend together. I guess this is good?" Jim looked at Tara for approval. She took the card to read, then admired the bottle. "Nice friends. Do we drink now or later?"

"Let's eat first." Jim kissed Tara on her cheek and then turned on the television. "Shall we watch something before we get ready for dinner?"

Tara nervously stood in front of the mirror of her room, adorned in a sleek, knee length pencil cut midi dress. Strapless on one side and off the shoulder long sleeved on the other, the salmon pink color paired with her tan skin magically. She wondered if the dress was over the top. She wanted to make an impression, though. She took in her silhouette in the mirror and felt like this dress held a secret key and a promise. The key that would unlock what she hoped would be a new level of intimacy with Jim. She knew what she wanted. She wanted Jim. She wanted him in her bed, hands all over her, inside of her.

Enough time had passed. They've known each other since elementary school, boyfriend and girlfriend in seventh grade, even though their relationship was cut short. They'd been dating for several months now. With that thought, Tara mustered her courage, reached for her clutch, and stepped into the living room. Jim stood at one of the windows, looking out at the sun dipping below the horizon, painting the sky with a warm sunset, casting a glow over the vineyards. Dressed in a fitted black suit which displayed his perfect ass, she stood watching him. He was so good looking. And he had a virtuous heart. She knew he cared for her. Maybe as much as she cared for him.

Jim felt Tara's presence. He inhaled, savoring the floral scent of her perfume. He turned to see her standing in front of him. He took her in. "God, Tara! You look," he paused, at a loss for words. "You look so damn good." Jim fought the urge to grab her and pull her in for a long, deep kiss. He wanted to walk her to his bed and forget dinner. He wanted to devour her.

"Thank you. You look damn good yourself. You ready?" At that moment, Tara felt rumbling in her stomach. When was the last time she ate?

Jim pulled Tara into him and gazed into her eyes. "I hope I can make it through dinner. I'm not gonna lie. If you said yes, I would take you to bed right now."

"Jim Stone. You promised me a five-star dinner," Tara said, flashing a playful smile.

"I did, but... we can order five-star room service, and I could take my time getting you out of that dress." Jim bit his lower lip, trying to control his urge to take her right there in the living room.

"Let's go." Tara locked her hand in his, walking out of their suite to the restaurant.

In the wake of a good bottle of wine and the best meal Tara thought she ever had, she intertwined her fingers with Jim's and they walked back to their suite. He turned to gaze into her eyes and gave her a heated smile as they walked to the elevator.

Jim pulled Tara close, leaned into her ear, and whispered, "Did I tell you how beautiful you look tonight?"

Tara lazily looked up at Jim, kissed him on his cheek, then nestled her head into his neck. "Yes, you did. You can say it again, though."

With eyes fixed on her and unwavering, Tara felt Jim was searching for something beyond the tangible, something that resided deep within the recesses of his soul.

Tara slowly licked her bottom lip, then whispered, "Tell me what you want, Jim."

Jim lowered his head to Tara's so their foreheads were touching. She felt his breath exhale, hoping he wanted what she did.

"I want you, Tara." Jim hugged her tightly.

Tara slowly pulled away from Jim, leading him to the door of their suite. She looked up at him, nodded, and waited for him to open the door. Hands interlocked, he led her inside. Within seconds, Jim's arms were around Tara, pulling her up and off the ground. She wrapped her arms around his neck, then her legs around his waist. He caressed his hands up her thighs, pushing up her dress. Their mouths came together, Jim softly kissing Tara. She took his face between her hands, kissing him deeply. The bottom of her dress now at her waist, Tara began to rock against Jim, feeling his hard length against her core.

"Tara, I don't think you know how long I've thought about this, about you." Not giving her a chance to respond, Jim claimed her mouth again with his lips and tongue. She tugged at his jacket as he planted open-mouthed kisses down her neck. "Hold on to me," Jim growled. As she hung onto him, he removed his suit coat and slowly walked them to his bedroom, laying Tara on his bed. He unwrapped her legs from his waist and stood.

"Are you okay?" Tara whispered.

With a mischievous glint in his eyes, Jim gave Tara a seductive smile that sent a shiver down her spine. "Are you sure?"

Tara gave him an inquisitive glance. "Sure about what?"

Several moments passed as they stared into each other's eyes with flaming heat. Tara spoke first. "Jim, I want you in every way I can have you."

Jim smiled mischievously, then said, "You're wearing too many clothes."

Tara's entire body hummed in anticipation as Jim pulled Tara to her feet and kissed her passionately. Her body tingled as he planted feather light kisses down the back of her neck and spine as he slowly unzipped her dress, watching it drop to the floor. She slowly turned to face him in only her black strapless bra and lace panties, cheeks flamed as she met his hungry gaze. "Now, *you're* wearing too many clothes."

Tara made quick work of unbuttoning and removing Jim's shirt, reveling in the grandeur of his chiseled chest. She stilled his hands when he reached for his belt buckle, locking eyes with his and took over unzipping his pants slowly. As they fell to the floor, she admired his hard muscular build and six-pack abs, gently trailing her fingers over his happy trail to the top band of his boxers. He swooped her up and took her to the bed, gently laying her down. Using his strength, he planked above her, getting lost in her dark, wanting eyes. Tara inhaled his clean, spicy scent and pulled him to her, licking his bottom lip before covering his mouth with a smoldering kiss.

Jim's hands roamed her breasts, his fingers tracing over her nipples through the lacy fabric. "Can I take this off?"

"Please," Tara panted.

Her breasts spilled out as her bra came off. Jim let out a moan, stroking them, lowering his mouth to her left nipple, his tongue drawing circles around it. Tara moaned in pleasure as he moved to the right nipple, sucking on it before taking a playful nip. He then blew a sweet breath over it to cool her skin. His hands slowly traveled between her breasts and down her stomach to stroke her center over her now wet panties.

"Jim. Please." Tara grabbed his hands to guide him to her pleasure.

He shifted down her body to kiss her inner thighs, before using his index fingers to wrap around her panties, pulling them down. "Tara. I can feel how wet you are for me."

She whimpered, her hands now entangled in his hair. He nestled his face to take her in with his tongue. He worshiped her, swirling his tongue, sucking on her clit, inserting one finger, then two to explore her walls. He knew she was close, feeling her body go stiff. Suddenly, her body seemed to splinter into a thousand shards of ecstasy.

"Jim!" Tara sighed.

He withdrew his fingers, slowly massaging her pussy. He looked up to her with a racy stare, then said, "You good?"

Tara released her hands from his now tangled strands, drawing him up to her. Her fingers began to explore his body, landing feathery strokes along the band of his boxers. She then began to draw soft circles along his lower hip, fingers crawling to caress his length. "Yeah, I'm good. And I'll be better when I have you inside me," Tara moaned before lifting her hips so her legs circled Jim's waist, pulling him close to her entrance. "I want all of you, Jim."

"You can have all of me, Tara." He reached over to the nightstand to grab a condom.

"Let me put it on," Tara demanded. She kissed his lips. Gaze stuck on him, she unwrapped the condom, throwing the wrapper to the floor. She motioned for Jim to lie on his back. She toured his upper body with her tongue, left hand massaging his balls. He let out a low growl when Tara took him into her mouth, circling his tip with her tongue. She released him, letting out a popping sound. Slowly, she rolled on the condom, then straddled him, lowering herself onto his length. His hands cupped her breasts as they moved in a rhythmic motion. In a swift move, never separating their link, Jim flipped them so she was on her back, lying underneath him.

Jim held her gaze as he slowly moved in and out of her. Each thrust filled her deeper, sending a wave of intense sensation through her body. In chorus, they both murmured, "Yes". He held her to the mattress for slow strokes and drugging kisses. He teased her nipples with his tongue as he moved in and out of her body. She wrapped her legs tightly around him, digging into his shoulders as she felt him move inside her. She clinched him, bringing her close to orgasm.

"I'm coming, Jim," Tara cried out.

"Baby, I got you. I want you to come again," Jim whispered in her ear.

Tara gasped as her body erupted into chills. A rush of pleasure jolted her, fierce and sizzling, like nothing she'd ever felt or imagined.

Not too far behind, Jim gritted out, "I'm coming, Tara." And he growled at the ferocity of the pleasure that ripped through him, an intense surge of joy and exhilaration that left him breathless. Their bodies tingled with delight, every nerve ending alive with a sense of profound happiness.

He stayed inside her for a while before pulling out, but stayed on top of her, relishing in the glorious moment.

Tara felt her heart was going to burst with emotion. A tear escaped from the corner of her eye. Jim lowered his lips to kiss it away.

"Jim?" Tara took a deep breath before speaking again. "I think I love you."

With a slight tilt of his lips, Jim kissed her lips softly. "I know I love you."

Tara never experienced anything like this, ever. This sensation was entirely new, wrapping her in a warmth and bliss that seemed almost otherworldly. Her heart raced as a shy smile spread across her face. "So, what do we do now?"

Without hesitation, Jim looked into her eyes and said, "We love each other. Forever."

Chapter 9

Dark Nights

In the weeks following their weekend together, Jim and Tara saw one another almost daily. Inseparable, their love for one another blossomed, their bond growing stronger with the passing of each twenty-four hours. Their conversations were a sanctuary, a place where they could share their hopes, dreams, and fears, without reservations. Ironically, their schedules synced, giving them the opportunity to share a cup of coffee or have lunch in between their respective patrolling of the streets and highways of Los Angeles.

At Captain Hanson's request, Tara entered his office at the start of her shift.

"Hello, Officer Phillips. I asked you to speak with me before your shift so that I could give you orders before you go out."

A sense of unease settled in the pit of Tara's stomach, a warning whisper that hinted to impending trouble. "Sir? Orders?"

Captain Hanson folded his arms across his chest and looked Tara in the eye. "Yes. I want you out on the 5 freeway looking for the sniper."

Tara needed to speak her mind. "Sir, with all due respect, I think that's out of our area. Isn't that up to the LAPD?"

"My orders are what they are. Do you have a problem with it, Officer Phillips?"

Despite her fears, Tara knew she had to abide by his orders. "No, sir. I'll head out now."

"Give me a report after your shift, before you leave," he barked.

Tara didn't answer. She knew this was wrong. She needed to gather more evidence before reporting Captain Hanson. In the meantime, she knew she was in danger. Once at her locker, she reached for her phone to text Jim.

> **Tara** - I'm on shift in thirty minutes. Got assigned to the 5 freeway to look for the sniper.

Jim responded moments later.

> **Jim** - I asked around. Some shots were fired two nights ago. No leads.

> **Jim** - I won't be far. If you need me or feel something is happening, text me, and our guys will come to you.

> **Jim** - Love you

> **Tara** - Love you too

Thirty minutes later, Tara took the on-ramp to the 5 freeway. Steering herself against what she was certain was an impending storm, she resolved to face whatever challenges lay ahead with courage.

An hour into her shift, Tara saw a stalled car ahead of her. She stopped behind the vehicle and radioed that she was stopping behind the car and recited the license plate. Exiting her car, one hand holding a flashlight, the other hand resting firmly on the grip of her gun still in the holster, she shouted, "Highway Patrol approaching." She flashed the flashlight into the backseat, then the front seat, noticing no one. As Tara slowly walked to the passenger side of the car, a sharp crack of gunfire pierced the air. She felt a searing pain tear through her right leg, sending shockwaves of agony through her body. She dropped to the ground, drew her gun, and quickly dragged herself to the driver's side of the car. She checked either side of where she sat, understanding she needed to get back to her patrol car. Tara needed to call for help. Despite the tortuous pain coming from her leg and burns from lugging herself on the prickly concrete, she pulled her walkie from her belt, pushed the call button and spoke. "Officer Phillips down. Shot by suspect assumed to be in the nearby bushes." She inhaled, then let out a hard breath. "Send backup and an ambulance." Tara knew not only would the nearest CHP come back her up, the LAPD would be notified. Taking in a deep breath, she managed to drag her body low to the ground to crawl to the driver's side of her vehicle. Through the haze of pain, Tara kept her gun drawn, ready to shoot should someone approach her. Waiting for help, she propped herself up against the left front tire. The pain was excruciating, a burning sensation that radiated outward in relentless waves. Her leg pulsed with each heartbeat. With every breath, her torment was amplified, making it nearly impossible to focus on anything other than the blinding, all-consuming pain. Finally, she saw LAPD lights.

The sound of police sirens grew louder, a high-pitched wail piercing the night air, while car headlights cut through the darkness, growing brighter as they approached the scene. The distant buzz of heavy engines transformed into a roar, signaling the arrival of reinforcements. Guns drawn as officers exited the squad cars, they immediately called out to who was presumed to be in the brush. Eyes now closed, Tara exhaled. As the voice drew nearer, a gush of recognition washed over her.

"Watch my back. I'm checking on the officer," Jim yelled as he ran to Tara. In that moment, she knew she had to act fast, to be his anchor so he wouldn't lose control at the sight of her.

With a steadying hand, she reached for him, doing her best to keep her voice calm as she spoke. "I'm okay. Can you stay with me?"

Jim dropped to Tara, embracing her. "Baby. Where were you hit?" He pulled away from her to survey her body. "Your leg!" Jim went into action, knowing he had to stop the bleeding and elevate her leg. Without a moment's hesitation, he gently but firmly lifted her leg, positioning it at an angle to minimize blood flow. He then applied pressure to her wound with his hand, working to stem the bleeding. Just as Jim was about to take off his shirt to apply more pressure to her wound, an EMT came up behind him.

"Officer? We can take it from here," the paramedic said.

She glanced over at him, gave him a wobbly smile and a thumbs up, then rested her head on the pillow the paramedic placed behind her head.

"Stone, we gotta go. Robbery in progress at the commercial building two miles back," Tyler warned. "More officers are now on scene. We gotta back up the one car at the building."

He kissed her forehead. "Tara, I'll be at the hospital as soon as I can." He knew Tara was in good hands now. Jim gathered himself and headed to the car, taking cleansing breaths to prepare himself for whatever was to come next.

Tyler and Jim arrived on scene to see several officers on site. They grabbed their bully sticks, hands on their guns, ready to go in.

"Several officers are on the premises, taking different floors in groups. There are several of them. Looks like a planned robbery," Officer Smith said. "Be careful. Take the lobby."

Jim heard Officer Smith radio they were coming in.

"Tyler, you go around that pillar. I'll take this side," Jim instructed.

Jim stood in place for a second to allow his eyes to adjust to the pitch-black darkness that was ahead of him. He didn't want to flash his light for fear of someone ready to attack or shoot him. Gun drawn, he slowly scoped the area. A few feet away was wall to wall glass. He couldn't move forward for fear of being a target, out in the open. Leaning up against the concrete wall, he inhaled before making a run for it. Just as he was about to bolt from his post, he heard three consecutive gunshots go off, followed by a loud thump to the ground.

"Fuck," he whispered. Lifting his walkie from his belt, he glanced right, then left before talking into his only line of communication with the officers outside the building. "Shots fired. Not sure who took the shots or if anyone was hit."

"Tyler?" Jim shouted. "Tyler, you good?" The area was ghostly silent, an eerie stillness settling over the scene. The sudden silence was thick and oppressive, amplifying the tension in the air. Jim knew at that moment, his partner was down.

Gun still drawn, he quickly moved in the direction he left Tyler. As realization dawned, a wave of anguish washed over him. Time seemed to slow to a crawl as he processed the situation. Tyler was lying there, still, not moving, blood pooling around his neck. Jim ran to him. With trembling hands, he reached out to his partner, desperation driving him forward. "Tyler, stay with me, man." Without a second more passing, he pressed talk on his walkie. "Officer James is shot, not mobile. Send an ambulance quickly." As the weight of the moment crashed down upon him, tears flooded Jim's eyes, blurring his vision with a torrent of emotion. He knew. Tyler was gone.

Chapter 10

Closure

Tara lay in her hospital bed, groggy from the surgery and medication. The sudden cognizance of weight at her feet alerted her to sit up. At the foot of her bed sat Jim, plopped in a chair, his upper body laying across her good leg. His closed eyes and the whistling of his snore confirmed he was asleep. Despite the chaos of the previous night, she found solace in the knowledge Jim was at her side. Tara lay her head back and closed her eyes, only to be jolted awake by Jim's loud moan.

"Jim? Are you okay?" Tara scanned his face, uncomfortable with the dark circles under his eyes. "Baby, I'll be okay. I shouldn't have any long-lasting effects from the bullet. My leg will be fine." She saw sorrow reflected in his gaze. His eyes, usually bright with determination, were now clouded with an unmistakable melancholy, revealing the depth of his emotions. "What's going on?"

Jim now held his shaking head in his hands as he spoke. "Tyler's gone. My best friend is gone." He tried to sniffle his tears away before looking at Tara.

With a look of fright in her eyes, Tara asked, "What do you mean?"

Jim stood, still wearing his uniform, and reached out for Tara's hand. He brushed his lips to her palm and kissed it. "After I left you, we had to rush to a burglary in progress. Tyler was shot by a suspect. He's dead."

Tara watched Jim's chest rise and fall in grief. His labored breath was heavy, a burden, as he struggled to come to terms with the devastating loss. The weight of sorrow seemed to press down on him, making it difficult to draw in air as tears welled in his eyes. His entire body trembled. Tara held her arms out, summoning Jim to her. "I'm so sorry, Jim. I know you and Tyler were close." They held each other for a while. In the quiet of the room, the only sound was the steady ticking of the clock, marking the passage of time with measured precision. In their shared embrace, they found refuge from the invasion of emotions swirling around them.

Tara and Jim both knew their chosen professions were hazardous. The demanding nature of the work, long hours, high levels of stress, and inherent dangers were challenging, especially when in a relationship. When they left one another, there wasn't a guarantee one would return. Being an office of law enforcement, whether protecting the highways or the streets and all that happened within a community, theirs was a dangerous job.

Tara toyed with his hair before speaking. "Jim? I don't know if I say this enough. But I love you."

"I love you more." Jim pulled her hand that caressed his hair and kissed her palm. "When you do this work, you sometimes forget the risks we take. Each time we are on duty, we place ourselves in harm's way. I don't want to take our moments together for granted."

Tara and Jim sat in silence for a beat. Tyler's death was a heavy weight to carry.

"We won't take our time together for granted. We'll cherish our time together and each other." Tara knew Jim would struggle with the death of his friend for a while. She was determined to support him through it all, just as she knew he supported her.

"I have to go back to the station and finish my report. I don't know all the details, but my thoughts are now with Nicole. I know she must be beyond herself." Jim stood slowly and kissed Tara on her forehead.

Tara wanted to be thoughtful with her next words. "I know I didn't get the opportunity to meet Tyler. Or Nicole. But what can I do?"

Jim took both of Tara's hands in his. "Baby, I don't know. What I know for certain is I need to be there for her. For Tyler's family."

"We'll be there for them, together. To be supportive of all of them."

With a heavy heart and a body weighed down by sorrow, Jim returned to the station to finish his report. He learned Tyler had entered an unlit closet. The suspect was lying in wait and shot Tyler in the neck on sight, hitting his jugular vein. He didn't have a chance to react. The suspect shot himself in the head after Tyler went down. The other suspects fled the scene only to be caught a short time later. It was all part of the job. Each time they went on a call, the chances of them not returning home were high. Tara's job was just as dangerous. He couldn't change what happened to Tyler. He couldn't bring him back. Tara was put in harm's way. Her injury was unwarranted. She shouldn't have been on that freeway staking out a sniper. He would do everything in his power to help with the investigation of Tara's captain and bring him down. That captain was wrong and would pay for his unethical orders.

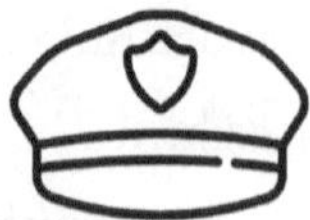

Two weeks later, Tara and Jim sat in the pew in the filled church to pay their respects to Tyler. Throughout the entire service, tears flowed, collective sobs echoing the room. Each tear, a testament to the love and loss of Tyler that weighed heavily on the hearts of all that gathered. Jim's captain walked to the podium to speak.

"Today, we gather to honor the life and service of a true hero, Tyler James. In the face of danger, he stood strong, embodying courage, integrity, and selflessness. His dedication to protecting and serving our community will never be forgotten. He may be gone, but his spirit lives on in the hearts of all who knew and loved him. Rest in peace, Officer James. Your sacrifice will never be in vain."

After the service, Jim sat head bowed, mourning his friend. Several minutes later, he glanced at Tara and stood. "Let's go." He helped Tara stand and handed over her crutches. He turned to his right and saw Nicole sitting in silence, head bowed, tears rolling down her face. "Give me a minute, Tara. I want to speak to Nicole."

Jim walked over to Nicole and sat down, reaching for her, and hugged her shoulders. "Tyler loved you, Nicole. With all his heart. I hope you know that. You have to believe that."

Nicole kept her head lowered, nodded and managed to give Jim a brief smile. "Thank you, Jim. I know that."

"Come on. Let's go. You shouldn't sit here alone." Jim reached for Nicole's hand to help her stand.

"You were a good friend to Tyler. You know that?" Nicole said softly.

"Yes, he was my best friend. You can ride with me and Tara to the grave site if you like."

Tears threatened to fall again. "Thank you, but my parents are here. I'll go with them."

With that, Jim held Nicole by her waist and supported her while she slowly left the church to join her parents and brother. "Call me if you need me, Nicole. You hear me?"

Nicole looked up at Jim and stroked his cheek. "Thank you. I will."

A month after Tara's shooting, the sniper was caught. The news reported he was concealed in the dense undergrowth beside the freeway, confident he would evade detection. The keen instincts and sharp eyes of law enforcement officers combed the area to pinpoint his location. They closed in on the sniper's location, moved in swiftly and stealthily to surround him. He attempted to flee, but in a matter of moments, the sniper was surrounded. He surrendered and was in jail awaiting trial for attempted murder of an officer of the law.

At the office of the California Highway Patrol, murmurs of discontent spread through the ranks, and complaints were filed against Tara's captain, casting doubt over his leadership. Allegations of misconduct and negligence swirled around the department, threatening the trust and confidence of those in charge. Calls for accountability rang out not just within the department but across the state once word got out about Tara's injury. As the investigation unfolded, the fate of the captain was terminal. He was fired a week after all findings went public.

Chapter 11

Two Hearts Becoming One

When released from the hospital, Jim insisted Tara stay with him until she could move around without assistance. Jim was off on bereavement and received therapy to process Tyler's death. He didn't want to let her out of his sight, fearing retaliation over her captain's firing. Temporarily living together brought love, laughter, and everyday moments that bound them together, making their relationship stronger. In the kitchen, they discovered the pleasure of cooking together, turning the often boring tasks of meal preparation into culinary adventures filled with laughter and experimentation. The scent of freshly brewed coffee and home-cooked meals filled Jim's home, inviting Tara to stay permanently. Sharing his house was not without challenges, navigating complexities of sharing space and balancing their individual needs and preferences caused friction. Open and honest communication and compromise saved them from the possibility of a breakup. Make up sex wasn't just about physical pleasure; it was a celebration of their love, a testament to the power of forgiveness and the strength of their connection.

A month after going home from the hospital, staying at Jim's for recovery, Tara was well enough to go home, to her own home. A stack of unopened mail awaited her as she entered her kitchen to prepare a cup of tea. Advertisements, credit card statements, and messages from realtors who wanted to list her house were the gist of her mail. As she reached the bottom of the pile, she noticed a red envelope addressed to her, in name only. There was no return address. Her address wasn't even printed on the envelope. Tara set it on the table as she took the steaming kettle off the burner.

"Honey, is everything in place? Do you need anything?" Tara's mom asked.

"I'm good, Mom. My mail is junk basically except for this red envelope."

Tara's mom smiled before asking, "What's in the envelope? Is it a letter? From who?"

A cup of green tea in one hand and a pastry in the other, Tara said, "Thanks, Mom, for the pastries." She sat down.

"I'm going to your room to change the sheets really quickly before I go."

"Thanks, Mom," Tara said, then opened the mystery letter.

Tara,

As I sit down to write this letter, I'm reminded of all the notes and letters we wrote to one another in seventh grade. My heart is filled with a love that words can barely express. With every beat of my heart, it whispers your name, a song of longing and devotion that resonates deep within my soul.

From the moment I stood under our favorite tree in the yard, and strung up the nerve to ask you to be my girlfriend, I knew you were something special. I thought I lost you forever. On that fateful day you stopped behind my car to rescue me from my flat tires, I knew you would be someone to change my life in ways I could never imagine. In your laughter, I found joy; in your kindness, I found solace; and in your love, I found home.

We took an oath to protect and serve the people of Los Angeles. Together, we drive the streets and highways, safeguarding the city. Like love on patrol, our lives are filled with adventure and excitement, un-predictability, and unwavering devotion. We stand side by side under an unprotected light, facing each day with courage and determination. At the end of each hard working day, we find comfort and peace in the safety of one another, united in our love and commitment.

As I pour my heart onto these pages, I find myself overwhelmed by the magnitude of what I'm about to ask. With trembling hands and a spirit filled with hope, I figuratively kneel before you, as a declaration of my unwavering commitment to cherish and honor you for all the days of my life.

I can't promise you a life from hardship and pain, but I can promise you this: that I will stand by your side through every storm, holding you close as we weather them together. Together, we will build a life of laughter, love, and endless adventure, a testament to the power of two hearts joined as one.

So, Tara, I ask you now with all the love in my heart. Will you marry me?

Yours now, and always,

Jim

Tears of love and joy flowed freely from Tara's eyes. Love spilled over from the boy she ran around the elementary school yard with, the adolescent she knew in seventh grade, to the man that captured her heart. From the innocence of childhood friendship and crushes, to the passion of adult romance, their love blossomed.

Tara stood, quickly scanning the room. "Where are my keys? Mom? I have to go to him."

"Go where, Tara?" her mom asked as she ran to the front door.

Tara grabbed her purse and opened her door to leave. As she took the first step, she was greeted by Jim, standing on her porch, hands in his pocket with that beautiful smile she loved so much. Behind him stood her dad, Jim's dad, her sister, and Sheridan. Jim turned to Tara, got on one knee and pulled out a red velvet box, then opened it to reveal the perfect, large white diamond, surrounded by smaller white diamonds, set in rose gold.

"Yes! Yes, Jim Stone, I will marry you." Tara rushed into his arms. With each press of their lips, they poured their hearts into the embrace and the kiss. Time stood still as they lost themselves in the intensity of the moment. They pulled away, breathless and flushed with emotion. Tara gazed into Jim's eyes and said, "I found my home in you. I love you."

To Tara's surprise, the sound of applause and cheers pulled her out of her bubble. She forgot about her favorite people that stood behind Jim. "You all knew about this?"

Jim pulled her close and said in her ear, "Tara. I love you and wanted everyone we care about to be a part of this moment." He placed the ring on her left ring finger, kissed it, then held her hand up for everyone to admire. "She said yes!" Jim said, facing their families.

"Jim? I'm going to be your wife."

"Tara? Yes, you are."

Epilogue

Nicole

Nicole held her best friend's hand and took a deep breath. "Aubrey? I can't do this."

"Yes, you can. I got you. We'll walk in together. Say congratulations, wish the happy couple well, then go get ice cream or something." Nicole softly chuckled at the mention of ice cream.

Nicole and Aubrey walked into the upscale steakhouse and followed the signs that read Jim and Tara's Engagement Celebration. The room was filled with an air of excitement. Nicole's heart fluttered with a mixture of joy and sorrow. Tyler should be with her at this moment, sharing in the joy of Jim and Tara's upcoming nuptials. It was a joyous moment, filled with laughter and warmth. Their faces beamed with happiness.

"Congratulations!" Nicole exclaimed. She enveloped them both in a warm embrace. Their eyes showed with so much love as Tara and Jim returned her hug.

Tara smiled and said, "Thank you so much, Nicole. It means so much for you to be here with us."

"We're over the moon!" Jim exclaimed. He took Nicole's hand. "How are you?"

Nicole did her best to give them a heart-filled smile. "I'm okay. I take it one day at a time." She waved Aubrey over to join them. "Jim. Do you remember my friend, Aubrey?"

"Yes, the chef. How can I forget all the delicious meals you fed Tyler and me on our lunch breaks? It's good to see you. Thank you for coming." Jim gave her a brief hug. "This is Tara, my fiancé."

Aubrey reached for Tara's hand. "It is a pleasure to meet you. Congratulations."

Nicole took Jim's and Tara's hands before speaking. "You both deserve all the love and happiness in the world. Tyler is shining down, celebrating with you."

Jim gave her hand a squeeze. "Please, Nicole. Stay and celebrate with us."

Aubrey glanced over to Nicole, reading her saddened expression. "We wanted to congratulate you in person. We wanted to be sure to share in this joyous occasion and say how happy we are for you both."

Jim pulled Nicole into an embrace and whispered, "You call me. Anytime."

Nicole nodded and blew kisses to Tara and Jim before turning to leave. With Aubrey at her side, they walked in silence to the car. Nicole placed her head in her hands. Her heart ached for Tyler. She let the tears fall down her cheeks, smearing the little makeup she had added to her face so she didn't look so depressed.

Aubrey took Nicole's hand. "Nicole. Each day, it gets a little easier. You may not feel it now, but I promise. You will be okay."

"I miss Tyler so much. We were supposed to be married." Nicole reached inside the glove compartment to grab a tissue to wipe her face. "Aubrey, how am I supposed to move on?"

"Girlfriend. You will, one day at a time." Aubrey stroked Nicole's hair. "And when you are ready, you'll love again."

Nicole blew her nose and let out a cleansing breath. "Love again? I don't know."

Aubrey turned Nicole's face to hers. "Trust me. You will."

About the Author

Kat Neil is a hopeless romantic and educator.
After many years as a reader of happily ever afters, she has plopped into the writing chair to craft love stories and main characters that make her swoon. When Kat is not writing, she is reading, shopping, or watching cooking shows.
She is a loving wife and mother to two amazing children.
She resides outside of Los Angeles, California.

Instagram – @katneilauthor
Website – http://katneil.com/

9 798990 565326